BEASTLY!

SNAKE SCARE

Andy Baxter

Illustrations by Brian Williamson

EGMONT

Special thanks to:
Glenn Dakin, West Jesmond Primary School,
Maney Hill Primary School and
Courthouse Junior School

EGMONT
We bring stories to life

Snake Scare first published in Great Britain 2008
by Egmont UK Limited
239 Kensington High Street, London W8 6SA

Text & illustrations © 2008 Egmont UK Ltd
Text by Glenn Dakin
Illustrations by Brian Williamson

ISBN 978 1 4052 3937 0

1 3 5 7 9 10 8 6 4 2

A CIP catalogue record for this title is available
from the British Library

Typeset by Avon DataSet Ltd, Bidford on Avon, Warwickshire
Printed and bound in Great Britain by the CPI Group

MAX MURPHY Becomes beastly anytime, anyplace, anywhere . . .

Absent-minded Uncle Herbert looks after Max and his twin sister Molly during term time while their parents are away.

MOLLY MURPHY
She's everything
Max isn't –
including normal!

Max longs for a normal family life,
but that's about as likely as his uncle
remembering which day of the week it is!

HERBERT SPLOTT
Mrs Murphy's batty
brother – otherwise
known as Uncle Herbert

Mr and Mrs Murphy are zoologists, so they're completely crazy about animals, and they're busy working on creating the best animal encyclopedia ever. Max thinks they're weird; who wants to stand around staring at sloths when you could be tucked up at home watching telly?

MR MURPHY AND MRS MURPHY
Very bright, but a little bit bonkers!
And completely clueless about
Max's secret . . .

PROFESSOR SLYNK
Mad, bad and dangerous
to know

And, as if all that didn't make Max's life tough enough, his parents' sinister colleague Professor Preston Slynk has found out his secret. Slynk's miniature insect-robot spies are never far away . . .

SNAKES: The Facts

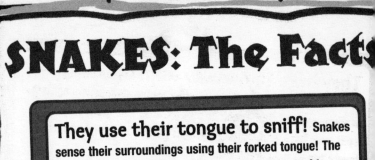

They use their tongue to sniff!
Snakes sense their surroundings using their forked tongue! The tongue collects particles in the air that are passed to a special organ in the mouth. This gives them a good idea of what something smells like. Clever, eh?

They can see through their 'eyelids'!
Snakes have 'brille' which are their version of our eyelids, made of a transparent scale. These come away with the skin when it's shed.

They never chew their food!
Snakes simply open their mouths wide (they have special jaw- and skull-bones that enable them to do this), and swallow whatever they're eating whole, head-first, so that it can't bite back before it goes down. Pythons can swallow animals as large as deer, pigs, and even crocodiles!

They have throwaway skin! To help them grow, snakes regularly moult their skin by rubbing themselves against something hard, like a rock or a tree trunk. This makes the skin split, peel back and fall off. Bleeugh! Underneath, the snake has lovely, brand-new, fresh skin!

They're as deaf as a post! That's because they have no ears – not that they care! Why would they, when they have special jawbones that can pick up vibrations? Cool!

They're toothy! Snakes don't use them to chew though, cos the teeth jut inwards to hook prey inside the mouth. A python can have as many as 200 teeth. Venomous snakes have grooves in their fangs to channel poison down from their venom ducts!

BRITISH ZOOS: The Fac[

- In Britain, there are over eighty mammal collections that can be classed as zoos

- London Zoo is the world's oldest scientific zoo, established in 1828. It was eventually opened to the public in 1847. Today, it houses a collection of more than 651 species of animals

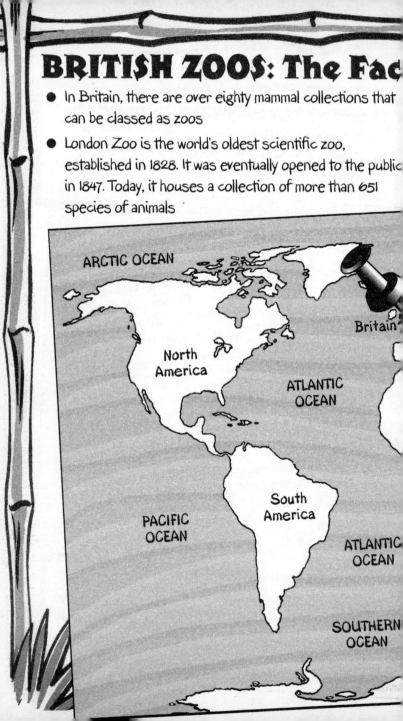

ARCTIC OCEAN

Britain

North America

ATLANTIC OCEAN

PACIFIC OCEAN

South America

ATLANTIC OCEAN

SOUTHERN OCEAN

- As well as being the first scientific zoo, London Zoo also opened the first reptile house (1849), first public aquarium (1853), first insect house (1881) and the first children's zoo (1938)
- Zoos in the UK are legally required to promote education and awareness of animal conservation

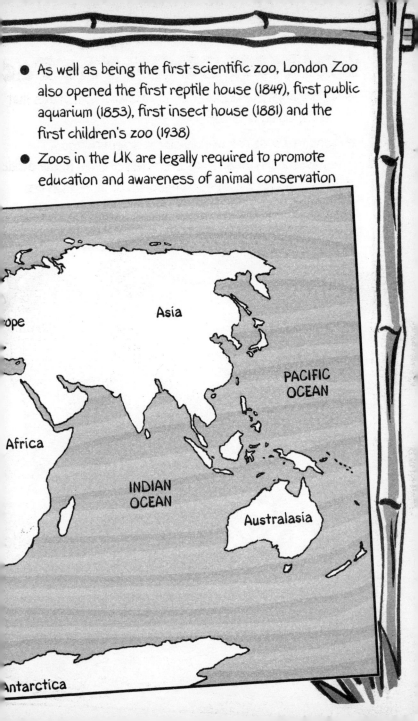

Contents

1. Going to the Zoo, Zoo, Zoo   1

2. Mad Max   12

3. Python Power   23

4. Sacked!   36

5. Stewart Stained   47

6. Cutting Remarks   57

7. Venomous Villainy   67

8. In the Tank   78

9. Smashing Time   88

10. Reptile Rage   98

Extra snake facts, jokes, quiz
and recipe!   109

***Monkey Mayhem* sneak preview**

1. Crackers Christmas   115

1. Going to the Zoo, Zoo, Zoo

The kitchen door crashed open, then was slammed shut with such force that Uncle Herbert's pictures swayed crookedly on their hooks.

'That's the *fifth* time he's been round the garden,' Molly exclaimed angrily. 'Even Professor Stink can't pretend he's here to watch the May blossom come out!'

Her twin brother Max joined her as she glared out of the kitchen window at a strange, scruffy creature, which seemed to be jumping from tree to tree in Uncle Herbert's big untidy garden.

'I know he's thick, but doesn't he realise people put scarecrows in fields, not gardens?' marvelled Max. 'That's the worst disguise yet. I'm going to start listing them and giving them marks out of ten.'

He sounded jokey but underneath he was deeply worried. Professor Preston Slynk – a zoologist, like the twins' parents – was desperate to find out how Max transformed into animals and would stop at nothing to be able to grab Max and take him to his private laboratory for tests.

'No point asking Uncle Herbert to get rid of him. He just wouldn't see the point,' gloomed Max.

'He just wouldn't *see* him,' added Molly. 'Even if he had three heads!'

Max felt suddenly cheerful at the vision of Slynk with three heads. He began happily drawing a picture of him in the margin of his geography homework with one hand, while shovelling down

a bowl of cornflakes with the other.

Molly stopped in her tracks. 'You're doing homework! Are you feeling all right? I thought you'd got a new computer game. I've never heard of *anyone* doing geography at breakfast time, specially you!'

'I forgot about it last week. Mr Miller said if I didn't give it in when I got to school, I wouldn't be able to go on the zoo trip,' he explained.

'Bor-*ing*,' said Molly. 'Anyway, I thought you didn't want anything to do with animals if you didn't have to.' It was bad enough, Max usually reasoned, to have to travel to various animal-packed countries around the world during the holidays, without having to see animals in school time, too.

Max's brow furrowed and he stabbed his geography homework with his biro. 'I want to know what makes my animal transformations happen,' he said. 'Is it because I'm thinking about it, or do I have to touch it, or what?'

'Can't be touching it,' said Molly. 'You didn't touch a mouse yesterday.' She grinned. 'Ahhh, you did look sweet!'

'You were just like Stink, trying to make me do tricks,' said Max furiously.

'I was *not*!' screeched Molly. She kick-boxed the

underneath of the table so that his homework flew into the air then landed in a messy heap on the floor.

Max shrugged. He wasn't enjoying the geography anyway. 'Hey, yesterday I slipped through a hole in the floorboards and found another of Uncle Herbert's secret rooms. If Stink manages to invade the house we can always hide in there.'

'If we can find the human way in,' said Molly gloomily. 'I couldn't squeeze into a tiny hole in the floorboards.'

Max had to admit he couldn't either, not while he was a boy anyway. But he'd really enjoyed looking at – and sometimes nibbling – all Uncle Herbert's mysterious objects stored in the attic and basement. 'I wonder where he got all that stuff from? What a pity I changed back just as Jake got here.' Molly had phoned his friend as soon as Max had transformed into a mouse, but Jake arrived too late to see more than a heap of mouse droppings.

Molly changed the subject. 'You can't go transforming at the zoo,' she instructed. 'What if Slynk follows you and grabs you?'

'He won't be there today,' boasted Max. 'And how would he know I was going on a trip?' Max grabbed a couple of slices of bread and began spreading peanut butter rapidly over them. 'Chuck over a couple of packets of crisps will you?'

'You may be ten minutes older than me,' retorted Molly, 'but I'm not your servant. Get them yourself.'

'Anyway, I'll have Jake with me when I transform,' went on Max. 'He'll cover for me.' He opened the fridge and eyed its contents. There was a dish of spaghetti with pink custard sauce over it (Uncle Herbert had made it for tea last night – there was rather a lot left), an open tin of sardines, some stale slices of cheese and a bag of green chillis. His hand hovered over the sardines, then came down on the chillis and a couple of slices of the cheese. 'So I'll be quite safe,' he finished. He found a knife on the draining board and began to carefully chop the chillis, scattering them over the peanut butter, then slapping the slices together.

'You can't eat peanut butter with chillis!' shrilled Molly.

'Why not?' said Max.

'Because . . . because . . .' Molly sighed. 'Changing into animals has changed *you* into a weirdo. What on earth will you turn into next?'

'A toothless squirrel,' beamed Uncle Herbert.

The children turned and gasped in horror. Molly had forgotten to keep her voice down when they were talking about her brother's transformations. How long had Uncle Herbert been standing there?

'Wh-what?' stammered Max.

'A toothless squirrel,' twinkled their uncle. 'Oh, sorry – I've done it wrong – that's the *answer*! What animal uses a nutcracker? That's what I should have said. I must get my riddles the right way round.'

He turned and shuffled out, muttering to himself as he went.

'That was close!' breathed Molly. 'Better not talk about zoos any more, just in case.'

'Suits me,' said Max, cross with Molly for always telling him what to do. He slid some of the stale cheese into his sandwich when she wasn't looking. He didn't want her going on about his strange diet again.

'I wish *we* were going to the zoo,' moaned Samreen.

As usual, the twins had called for their best friends on their way to school.

'Tell you what, we'll do something else instead,' said Molly.

The two girls bent their heads together and giggled their way along the road.

'Do you reckon you might transform at the zoo?' whispered Jake. He was the only one of the twins' friends who knew about Max's strange ability, though he still wasn't sure whether to believe it or not. 'How did you change into that mouse yesterday? Do you have to think your way into it? Or trip over a pile of poo or something?'

'I didn't think about mice yesterday,' said Max. 'I was thinking about *Space Ninjas* and doing my homework . . . Oh, no! I've done it and I haven't brought it with me!' He emptied the contents of his bag out all over the pavement.

10

'Oh, yes, I have.' He sighed with relief and grinned at Jake.

As he repacked his bag, Max saw something out of the corner of his eye. Well, not something – someone. It was an old lady with a walking frame. A really gross old lady, with wiry grey hair sticking out of her headscarf, and monster warts all over her chin.

'Look out,' he giggled, 'there's an old witch behind us!'

The old lady was covering the ground very fast, even with the help of her walking frame. Surely she couldn't be . . .

He had to give Slynk top marks this time – if it hadn't been for the super-speedy walk, he really would have been fooled!

2. Mad Max

Max nudged Molly. No words needed to pass between them. Molly could tell from the mixture of dismay and disgust on her brother's face that they were in a Serious Slynk Situation!

Max was desperate to lose Slynk. On the one day he actually wanted to change into an animal, he couldn't let the professor get in his way.

'Down here,' Max said, turning aside from their usual route to lead his friends down a grimy back alley. Soon they were hopping over puddles and weaving between stray shopping trolleys. Maybe he could shake Granny Slynk off, without having to explain his arch-enemy to his friends.

'Ah, the scenic route!' remarked Samreen, pulling a face as she stepped over a split rubbish bag.

'This way's quicker,' said Molly, taking Max's lead and cutting through the back yard of the local burger bar. The stink of stale grease hit her nostrils as they passed the kitchen door.

'Love that smell,' sighed Max, his eyes closed in rapture. He grinned as he ducked through a hole in the fence and led them across a building site, down a smelly subway, and across the supermarket car park. They were almost at the school gates.

Glancing around, Max could see no sign of Slynk, but that didn't prove anything. His enemy was getting more cunning all the time, and like a bad smell, he was very hard to shake off.

Max was relieved to see the huge cream-coloured coach waiting in the school car park. He was even pleased to see old Mr Knocker beckoning him and Jake on board.

Molly shouted goodbye as Max disappeared inside. She felt a sudden pang of fear, mixed with envy, at the thought of her brother heading off on a day of adventure without her. Despite herself, she gave a final call of, 'Be careful!' Hoots of laughter erupted around her, as the rest of Max's class piled aboard the coach.

'Be careful in that big scary zoo!' mocked Paul Parnell, slimy sidekick to school bully, Stewart Staines. 'Watch out for those nasty penguins!'

For once, Molly had no clever comeback. The other kids were lucky. They would never know how a fun day out could turn into a life-or-death adventure, but it was a fact of life for Max.

Max had nabbed a window seat and was just

about to give Molly a superior big-brotherly wave when he froze in horror. Professor Slynk, still grannied-up and pushing his walking frame was climbing on to the school coach.

There's no escape, thought Max. Slynk's beady little eyes seemed to be flashing at Max, as his freakish figure lurched up the steps. *How the heck did he know I was going on a trip?*

'Now now, grandma,' grinned the coach driver, a red-faced man in an enormous maroon blazer. 'This isn't the seventy-three, you know!' The burly driver propelled Slynk down the stairs.

'But – but . . .' squawked Slynk in protest.

'Yes, you'll be wanting the city-centre shuttle,' the driver said, taking Slynk by the arm. 'It's a big green bus.'

'No, no!'

'Poor old dear's a bit deaf I expect,' muttered the driver, and Max chuckled as Slynk was

15

dragged away with the driver bellowing the words 'big' and 'green' in his ear continually.

A schoolbag went flying over Max's head, hurled by none other than Stewart Staines. Max glanced down at his feet to make sure the bag hadn't been his own. Good, it was still under his seat. But there, by his shoe, was a tiny, crab-like robot pointing a miniature camera lens up at him. It looked all too familiar.

Max knew what to do. His trainer came down on it with a satisfying crunch. He ground his heel on the broken metal pieces with a smile. Sighing happily, he lay back in his seat. No Professor Stink, no robot spies and no school work. It was time to get down to the serious business of the day – swapping football cards with Jake.

'If Earth United ever play the Moon, this is the World Team they'll pick,' Max boasted, proudly flicking through his cards one by one.

'Yeah, and they'll lose,' said Jake. 'Even though there's nobody on the moon to play them! Now check out my Dream Team . . .'

A strange feeling took hold of Max, a feeling he didn't at first recognise. Then he realised what it was: the simple, everyday happiness of just being an ordinary boy enjoying ordinary life. The feeling didn't last long.

A big pink hand snatched Max's cards away

and tossed them in the air, scattering them all over the bus. The culprit, Stewart Staines, roared with laughter.

'What's up, Murphy?' taunted Paul Parnell. 'We thought you liked collecting cards – you can collect 'em all up again now!'

The bus went silent. Everyone watched. They were waiting for Max to go down on his hands and knees, grovelling under seats to get his precious cards back, pretending to find the prank funny, as Stewart's victims usually did. But that didn't happen.

'OK,' Max sighed, looking across at Jake. 'As well as chucking my cards around, Stewart has already flicked bogeys at Jenny Jones, and emptied a bottle of water over Hannah Harper's designer bag . . .'

'Yep,' said Jake, 'and we're not even out of the school gates yet!'

'Mr Knocker's too busy gassing with the bus driver to care about what's happening back here,'

Max added. 'If someone doesn't do something now, this trip – this whole day – is going to be ruined by one moron!'

Then, to Jake's complete astonishment, Max did the unthinkable. He got out of his seat to confront the bully face to face.

He advanced on Stewart, who was standing in the coach's central aisle.

'Pick up those cards!' ordered Max. The bully looked lost for words. He wasn't used to being spoken to like this. But Max was strangely calm.

'It was only a joke,' sneered Paul Parnell, slouching in the back seat.

'I'm not talking to you, Small Paul,' Max replied. There was a giggle from Jenny Jones. Paul went red.

Max took another step towards Stewart. 'I was talking to your mate,' he said in a loud voice for all to hear, 'Brain Strain.'

The whole class held its breath. Using Stewart's nickname to his face was the ultimate crime. But the bully just stared at Max gormlessly.

'Tell him,' grunted Stewart, turning to Small Paul for support. He jabbed a fat thumb towards Max. 'Tell him what he'll get!' Paul peeped up over the seat.

'You won't like it!' he warned Max.

'That's not telling him!' moaned Stewart. 'That was rubbish!'

Max laughed.

'Don't strain your brain, Brain Strain,' Max said. 'You're pathetic. You can't even think up your own threats!'

Max was enjoying himself now, and all kinds of insults floated through his mind. He could get a good laugh by suggesting that Stewart was going to visit his closest relatives at the zoo, but he doubted Brain Strain would even understand the joke.

Smiling, and confident he could crush his foe with a few well-chosen words, Max glanced across at Jake to make sure his friend was enjoying the big moment. Big mistake.

In that split second Stewart attacked and a meaty fist sent Max flying half way up the bus.

3. Python Power

'That's enough!'

The fact that Max Murphy had just landed in the middle of Mr Knocker's battered old road atlas of Britain, finally convinced the teacher that it was time to take a firm hand.

'The next pupil to make a noise will have the pleasure of my company for the whole day!' he barked. Mr Knocker may not have been the sharpest pencil in the box, but he did know that a day of his bird-watching tips and advice on how to speak proper English wasn't anyone's idea of a good time.

Max's world was still on spin cycle. He staggered to his feet and somehow clambered back to his seat next to Jake without really being very sure of which way was up.

'Nice going,' said Jake. 'You just tried to take on the school psycho – and his evil sidekick – single-handedly, on a moving bus, within centimetres of nutty old Knocker. Are you trying to win Idiot of the Year?'

Max grinned. 'I was just about to spring back into action and take them both out when Knocker stopped me,' he said, trying to guess from his faint reflection in the coach window whether or not Stewart had given him a black eye.

Jake spoke even more quietly now, and Max could see real concern in his friend's bright brown eyes.

24

'What's with the whole death-wish thing?' Jake asked. 'Those animal transformations must be messing with your mind!'

Max fell silent. Jake might be right. The old Max, the normal Max, knew a hundred-and-one ways to stay out of trouble and laugh off the antics of idiots like Brain Strain. But back there he had felt different, stronger, more able to take command of a situation.

'Maybe,' Max whispered, as the whole coach gradually forgot Mr Knocker's threat and the usual crazy hubbub returned. 'Maybe I did feel something . . . a kind of animal pride, like I wasn't going to back down.'

It was an intriguing but scary thought. Could the animals he had turned into be leaving traces of their instincts in his brain? He felt a sudden urge to eat the stale cheese sandwiches in his lunch box, but fought it back. Was he a man or a mouse?

'Did you think you were King of the Jungle when you stood up to Brain Strain?' laughed Jake. He nodded towards the bully. 'That guy is the animal – not you!'

In the street, not far behind them, passing pedestrians were puzzled as some tatty women's clothes and a ratty grey wig flew out of the window of a big black jeep that was following the coach.

For once it was going to be easy, Slynk told himself as he pushed his disguise out of the car window. So far he had gone completely unnoticed! In fact, his old-lady act had been so good he was sure that one old codger outside the school gates had been about to ask him out on a date.

'Today is *my* day!' he cackled, his narrow eyes glinting wickedly behind the grubby lenses of his round spectacles. 'That wretched Murphy boy is actually visiting the zoo! It's too perfect! He's sure to use his powers!'

On previous occasions, he – the world's great robotics scientist – had been forced to hunt his prey in strange, unpredictable, faraway places; dangerous jungles and swirling oceans. This time, Max Murphy was on home ground in a nice local zoo, conveniently close to Slynk's private rooms at The Academy. Rooms from which no animal ever emerged alive.

Glorious sunshine slanted down through the fibreglass palm trees shading the main gate of the zoo. Max stretched his cramped limbs after the

long and stuffy coach trip and nudged Jake to one side. He handed his friend a plastic bag.

'Here are some spare clothes I might need later, in case I get separated from my school uniform during the transformation,' he said. 'Stuff them in your bag and keep a lookout either for an animal waving at you, or me running around starkers!'

Jake stowed the plastic bag in his backpack. 'What if you don't transform in time to catch the coach home?' Jake worried.

'I should be back to normal by then,' Max reassured him. 'But if I'm not, I'll need you to cover for me.'

'But how will you get back?' asked Jake, anxiously.

'I'll find a way,' said Max. 'But don't fret, it's not going to come to that.'

Max looked around at the cages and bird houses on all sides. Now was the time to make the big decision.

'World of the Gorilla?' he suggested, pointing at a signpost in front of him.

'What about Palace of the Penguins?' suggested Jake, 'or Kingdom of the Komodo Dragon?'

Exciting possibilities abounded on all sides. Max was trying to feel as light-hearted as his friend, but deep down there was that twinge of fear – that sense of diving into unknown waters.

Was it a mistake to try and bring on the

change deliberately, just to see if he could? Was it a misuse of his rare ability? And how on earth could he choose which animal to become?

The decision was soon made for him. Mr Knocker was sounding off nearby.

'As I want this to be an educational and informative occasion, I have hired a guide to accompany us,' the teacher was droning. 'I'm delighted to introduce you to our expert today, Miss, um . . .'

'Fred Flinders,' perked up a voice with a broad Aussie accent. Max was amused to see that Fred was a pink-haired girl with a pierced nose and a goth T-shirt visible under her safari jacket. She clearly was not what Mr Knocker had expected.

'I beg your pardon?' he protested. 'How can your name be Fred if you're a girl?'

'Short for Winifred, mate!' she replied. 'Don't like being called Winnie – makes me sound like a startled horse. Now, all follow me!'

Fred led the group into the reptile house. Illuminated tanks stretched far away into the cool darkness.

'Reptiles rock!' shouted Fred gesturing all around her. 'Reptiles rule! They're wild and cool!' she added in a kind of chant.

Mr Knocker groaned and rubbed a hand through his thinning hair.

'Oh, dear, Winifred,' he said. 'Do animals really have to be "cool"?'

Everyone laughed. Meanwhile no one had noticed a squat figure slip through the door behind them, and waddle into the gloom beyond.

'You!' Fred suddenly cried out, pointing straight at Max. Max blushed to the roots of his blonde hair. He held his breath. Did Fred somehow know about him and his powers? But the guide just smiled.

'Does your mum hate it when you gobble things

31

up in one bite?' she asked. There was more laughter, while Max tried to suck in his podgy stomach.

'Yep,' said Max.

'Well, she would hate snakes then,' Fred said, 'because they swallow their tucker in one gulp! Did you know a python can swallow a child whole and then digest it in its guts for a couple of weeks? After that, the gorged snake won't have to eat again for almost a whole year! Cool or what?'

There was a murmur of approval. Fred led the pupils further into the chamber. But Max lingered behind, gripped by the sight of the creatures in the python tank. Behind the glass pane, a diamond-spangled python several metres long was uncoiling its body and gliding slowly in and out of the shadows. There was something hypnotic about it.

Nearby, Fred was holding up a snake skin in her outstretched hands and inviting the class to come and stroke it.

'You'll be amazed,' she said. 'It's not slimy and gross, it's smooth and dry.'

Jake followed the crowd. Max didn't. He had started to get a weird taste in his mouth. His scalp was prickly and his skin was as dry as paper. Suddenly, he felt a shock of cold as if someone had dropped him into a bucket of icy water. A sharp pain burned the tip of his tongue, as if it were splitting in two. He tried to cry out, but all he could force from his throat was a rattling hiss.

Panic almost gripped him as he felt his arms pin to his sides, his fingers melt away and his legs stick together and lose all sensation.

With a *thump* he tumbled to the floor, his vision blurred but still revealed his own silvery-grey coils. He was a snake. And not just any snake – he had become a python!

Before he could untangle himself from his school clothes he saw the most unwelcome sight

in the world. Professor Slynk, his eyes glowing with triumph, was bearing down on him with a big sack.

4. Sacked!

There was no escape. Determined hands in thick leather gloves bundled Max up with his school gear and thrust him straight into the sack. Before Max's head disappeared, he caught a glimpse of Jake looking around wondering where he had gone.

'Jake!' Max tried to shout, but once again, his forked tongue could only hiss.

'Max?' Jake peered through the gloom in all directions but there was no sign of his friend. All

Jake could see was a rather strange man who seemed to be having trouble carrying a sack of laundry. Bizarrely, the laundry appeared to be wriggling about with a life of its own. The man didn't seem bothered at all, in fact he was rather puffed-up and delighted about something.

'Max?' Jake called quietly, turning his back on the sackman, who was quickly heading for the door.

'Max!' Jake shouted, feeling that he had missed a trick somehow – that something was wrong.

Max's serpent senses were revolted by the reeking, stuffy confines of the hessian sack. His own underpants weren't exactly a bunch of roses either. Max felt furious. He writhed, heaved and wriggled his elongated body around with all his might.

Come on, you idiots! Somebody must be able to see this! he wanted to shout.

Slynk grunted, cursed and gripped the sack more tightly. Max heard Jake's voice growing fainter as his friend hunted for him in the wrong direction. Max knew he had to do something fast. He wiggled, curled and looped his body in an amazing outburst of serpentine gymnastics. He was hoping to put on such a frenzied display that someone, maybe Mr Knocker or even Fred the zoo guide, would stop Slynk and question him about his haunted laundry bag.

'Stop right now!'

Max's heart leapt as he heard the familiar roar of his teacher's voice. *Good old Mr Knocker,* Max thought. *Eagle-eyed, on-the-case, have-a-go-hero, Mr Knocker.*

'I can't take you anywhere, can I, Staines?' Mr Knocker's voice continued. 'Put that dead mouse back in the feeding bucket, get outside and wait for the class by the back door!'

39

Max's hopes came crashing down. Dismayed, he stopped struggling and his body went slack. Slynk chuckled and took this as a sign that Max had given up.

'I see you're starting to get the idea!' Slynk growled through the thick fibres. 'You're trapped, helpless – it's all over!'

They were now leaving the reptile house. Although it was dark in the sack, Max found that snakes had other ways of picking up information than just by using their eyesight. Every vibration from Slynk's heavy footsteps told a tale: what kind of surface he was walking on; how near to a doorway he was; how fast or slow he was going.

He heard Slynk's boots clicking on the stony floor. With his tongue he tasted – or was it scented? – a change in the air inside the sack. Next they were outside, heading somewhere fast. Max didn't have time to marvel at the fact that he could now smell things with his tongue. He had to find a way out of this mess.

I should always stay hidden, his snake instincts warned him, *never let the enemy see me!*

Max knew he had been too careless. Now he needed to get to grips with his new animal features, but somehow let his human side stay in control.

Slynk pressed his pink lips up to the sack and whispered into it.

'You've led me a merry dance up to now, Max, but at last it's over – especially since you haven't got any feet to dance with!' he cackled.

Disgusting, Max thought. Not that rubbish joke, but Slynk's breath. Max's tongue could smell fatty sausages, sugary ketchup and oily fried bread – all the signs of a massive fried breakfast, topped off with a dose of cheap mouthwash. *Gross!*

'I'm not a cruel man,' Slynk continued. 'I'll

inject you before I put you on the slab. You won't feel anything while I slice you up and learn your secrets.'

A tense, cold fury possessed Max's whole body, seeming to travel up and down his spine like icy electricity.

I'm a survivor. I can get out of anything, Max told himself. *Nothing can hold a python!*

'Sadly, I can't explore all your interesting bits and still leave you in one piece, of course,' Slynk chuckled. 'So I'm afraid it's time to wave goodbye to all your friends. Oops – sorry, you've got no hands to wave with either!' he guffawed. 'Pretty useless being a snake isn't it?'

Max felt ready to explode with rage but he was amazed at his cool self-control. He would save his anger and strength until an opportunity came. Patience, cunning, waiting – that was the way of the snake.

Slynk was huffing and puffing along for all he was worth. Max could now hear the happy chatter of a chimp. They must be passing Monkey Land now, dangerously close to the zoo exit.

Suddenly, Max heard footsteps racing towards him. His hopes lifted again. Was this Jake, rushing to the rescue?

Whump! There was an almighty collision. There were cries of pain and surprise. The sack thumped to the ground. Max shot out like a bolt of slithery lightning and hid under a nearby bench.

'Look where you're going, four-eyes!' came a familiar, sneering voice. It was Brain Strain! Stewart had been running around outside like the idiot he was, and had accidentally flattened Slynk!

Red faced, the bully was soon on his feet, only slightly winded. But Slynk was still on the ground. He had apparently banged his head in the fall

and was out for the count. Max was so delighted to be out of the tight sack, he stretched his serpent body out to its full length, enjoying his freedom.

Well, well, thought Max, *even an idiot like Stewart comes in handy occasionally!* He was just wondering whether he might have misjudged Brain Strain a little, when he heard a sudden, sharp clang followed by a shriek from the chimps.

Max slithered out from under his bench and

slunk through the grass to get a better view. At first, he found the sunlight a bit dazzling.

Just my luck, Max thought. *Snakes don't have proper eyelids! Maybe that's why they like lurking in the shadows.* He gradually adjusted to his snake vision and saw Small Paul and Brain Strain outside the chimp enclosure.

'Don't you hoot at me like that!' Stewart snarled at the bewildered creatures. 'I suppose you think it's funny I crashed into that old geezer!' He hurled a handful of stones at them. The chimps went wild, bounding from branch to branch. Max was disgusted. Wasn't it bad enough that the animals were trapped behind bars, without chucking things at them too?

Nice distraction though, his snake side observed. *The perfect chance to slip away unnoticed.*

'Look at them jump!' Stewart snorted with laughter. Small Paul joined in, pulling a couple of empty cans from the nearest bin.

'This'll make them squeal!' he cackled. He hurled the cans against the bars, scaring the chimps into a frenzy. Stewart started throwing handfuls of dirt, pebbles, anything he could grab. Small Paul's high-pitched giggle set all Max's scales on edge. The rotten behaviour of his two classmates made Max feel embarrassed to be human – whichever part of him was still human. Max decided he couldn't just hide there and watch helplessly, he had to act.

He gazed at his long, limbless form and felt at a loss. *No arms, no legs . . .* he thought over all the snags of being a snake. *What on earth can I do?*

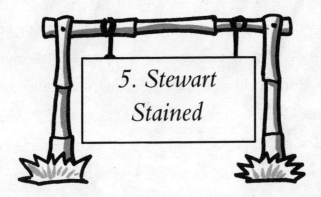

5. Stewart Stained

'Hey! Not fair!' whined Small Paul. Max glanced up through the leaves. While he had been bemoaning his lack of useful body parts, the chimps had started to fight back!

A grizzled old chimpanzee had picked up an armful of rotten fruit and was hurling banana skins through the bars. *Slap!* A slimy skin left a nasty smear on Small Paul's ear. For a moment, Max thought Paul was going to cry. Stewart roared with laughter.

'Har, har – Paul Parnell, beaten by a monkey! I've never seen anything so funny – hey, watch it!' Stewart's glee was cut short by a shower of twigs landing on his head. A young chimp, swinging backwards and forwards on a tyre, had found a nice high vantage point from which to bombard his human foes.

'Woo-hoo-ha-ha!' The chimps bounced up and down and bared their teeth gleefully. Then they swapped places and seemed to slap each other in passing.

'Of all the –' Stewart was about to blow his top, 'I'll swear they just high-fived each other!'

'That means they think they're winning,' snivelled Small Paul, his green eyes narrowing. He knew how to get his revenge on the chimps – by winding up Stewart.

'That jumping up and down thing they're doing,' Paul continued, 'it's a kind of victory dance. They'll be showing you their butts next! It's the ultimate insult in the animal kingdom.'

'Oh, they will, will they?' Stewart snarled. 'Victory dance, is it? Well, now they're going to lose – big style!'

Stewart started scrabbling in the flowerbeds. He soon came back to the cage with filthy hands and a pile of stones to lob at the caged animals. Max raised his flat head from the grass and looked round in all directions. As this was a school day the zoo was quiet and there was no real help on hand at all. The only human in sight was Professor Slynk, and he was still unconscious.

The enemy is looking the other way. Time to strike! Max reared up his head and bared his fangs. He flicked his tongue over his four rows of teeth. Pythons weren't venomous – there was no danger of him actually *killing* Brain Strain. But he could certainly give the big bully a chomp he would remember all his life. He slithered forward and reared up to strike . . .

What on earth am I doing? Max suddenly thought. He dived into the long grass again, clamping his scaly lips tightly shut. *I can't just chomp someone because they're behaving badly – I've got to rise above my animal instincts!* And in any case, there was no way he wanted to put his mouth anywhere near Stewart's chubby legs.

It would be so easy to bite him, Max thought.

But no, Max told himself. *There has to be another way.* Just then he saw the cheeky younger chimp looking around the cage for something new to throw. The animal's eyes fell on a big, steaming pile of . . .

Oh, yes, thought Max, with a twinkle in his eye. *Go for it!*

As the chimpanzee scraped up a big handful of warm, stinking dung, a plan began to form in

51

Max's mind. A plan sneaky enough to satisfy even his snake instincts.

It was time to act. Max broke cover and shot through the grass towards the enclosure. Before Stewart knew what was happening, he had several metres of rippling python wrapped tightly round his shins. He went white, gasped and his eyes almost popped out of their sockets in disbelief. Then he screamed for all he was worth, struggled and tried to kick out – but it was no good. Max was a very long, very strong snake, and keeping a tight grip on an enemy was one thing he could do as a python better than any other creature.

The chimp advanced right to the front of the enclosure, cackling and capering. He drew a strong furry arm back, took careful aim and let fly.

SMACK! The chimp poo hit Stewart square in the eye, easily as hard as the bully had punched Max earlier. Hissing with laughter, Max released

his coils so that Brain Strain was free to fall backwards on his bottom and howl with disgust as he wiped away the warm orange poo.

It dribbled down his face and on to his school uniform, dripping on to his crisp white shirt and spattering his pale grey trousers.

'Wow!' gasped Small Paul, hardly able to believe his eyes. 'What a shot! I mean – what a pity! I mean . . .' he gave up trying to keep a straight face and started to snigger.

Careful, Paul, Max thought as he watched the fun from under a bush, *Brain Strain will make you pay for that later!*

But Max had made a big mistake. He had been enjoying the fun far too much to pay attention to what was happening behind him. Groggy, dribbling from the corner of his mouth, and with the fine babyish hair above his forehead matted with blood, Professor Slynk was finally rising to his knees.

Slynk's head hurt – it felt like it was splitting. There was a sound of laughter, chimpanzees hooting and howling. Those happy sounds made Slynk mad. Someone was going to pay for this! Frantically, he fumbled around until he found his fallen glasses. Snarling with rage, he stuck them on his nose and gazed around him.

At first he was seeing double, but he blinked

again and everything became clear. Everything became *very* clear. There, in the grass just in front of him, was a familiar-looking python – and it hadn't spotted him.

'Gotcha!' he roared, shoving Max back into the sack. He swung the bulging bundle across his back and raced straight for the exit.

Max felt like he was tumbling about in a washing machine. He cursed himself over and over again for his stupidity in taking his mind off Slynk even for a moment.

'You had your chance,' shouted Slynk, not caring who heard him. He threw the sack on to the hard tarmac of the car park and trod down the top with one big boot, while he fumbled in his pocket for a piece of twine.

'You had your miraculous escape, like you always do! But now it's over! You've used up your confounded luck. This time I win!'

Slynk tied up the bag. Max heard a click as the car boot opened and he was thrust inside. The door slammed.

'Yes!' exulted Slynk, as if he had just scored the winning goal in the World Cup final. 'I've done it at last! Nothing can stop me now!'

Max heard the throaty rumble of the jeep starting up. They were off. Miles droned by in pitch darkness. He could only lie and wait, hearing Slynk's words echoing in his brain. *This time I win . . .*

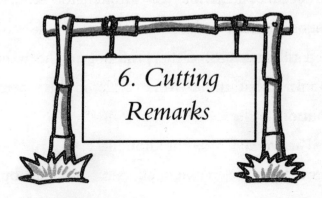

6. Cutting Remarks

Flexing his muscular coils with all his might, Max tried to force his way out of the bag. The string at the top of the sack had to be the weak spot. Slynk was a bungler – he was not Doctor Diabolical, the Most Evil Genius in the Cosmos (who was always outsmarting Max in his new computer game).

Max corkscrewed his long tail to create a kind of spring, then launched himself towards the top of the sack. Ouch! He only succeeded in catapulting the whole bundle, including himself, into the side of the car. The twine was knotted too securely. Maybe Professor Slynk had been a boy scout. Even the thought of the professor in shorts and woggle didn't make Max smile in his current situation.

What an idiot I am! he thought.

Stuck in the stinky sack, Max had plenty of time to blame himself for his own dire situation. Why hadn't he listened to his snake instincts when they had told him to sneak away while he had the chance?

Because it was so cool to see Brain Strain get what he deserved, Max told himself. He knew he had done the right thing in helping the chimps to fight back. In order to keep control of his animal side he had to think like a human, not give in to his snaky instincts.

Wait — what was that? Max felt a faint tickle in

his sensitive underbelly. The sensation meant there was movement nearby – something else was in the car boot!

Suddenly, little legs were scurrying all over the sack. It gave Max the creeps. What could be in there with him? He felt a rush of fear, fear of an unknown presence, maybe an enemy. He wriggled to shake the intruder off, but it was pointless. The little legs were soon running all over him again, more of them this time.

He was about to panic when he realised his tongue was detecting a metallic odour. Then, in the pitch dark, Max could gradually make out a couple of pale blobs of light moving around. His snake brain told him he was seeing the blobs with special heat sensors in slits beneath his eyes. The light he saw was actually the heat of tiny power cells. Those moving objects were Slynk's little robots, spying on his every move!

Oh, no! His enemy's eyes were everywhere, even here in the car boot where he'd been hoping to pull off a daring escape! Max hated feeling so helpless, it made him seethe with anger.

It aroused his reptile rage, too. He felt his muscles expanding and contracting with a desire to squeeze and strangle and crush and kill. Biting would be good, too. Right now, he'd give anything to be able to strike back.

For a split second, Max's snake-self won and, in a blind fury, he sank his fangs into the side of the sack.

At first, it felt wonderful just to bury his teeth into something, but then came the realisation that he had made another blunder. Now his fangs were stuck in the thick hessian of the bag. He had trapped himself even more thoroughly than Slynk had.

Well, that was clever, Max thought gloomily. He curled himself up into a miserable heap and waited helplessly.

The car stopped. He felt the bag being hauled out of the boot. It jolted his fangs, where they were caught in the sack.

Slynk carried the sack across another car park. He heard the chimes in The Academy clock tower close by and knew exactly where he was going. It made him feel cold inside. Slynk's private

61

rooms. The horrible laboratories that, up until now, he and Molly had only joked about.

He heard doors opening and shutting, the drawing of bolts. His sack was placed on a metal slab – he could smell it, taste it, feel the antiseptic cold.

'You just wait there,' Slynk muttered. 'I must prepare for my glorious exploration of your delicate inner workings. Now where are my scalpels?'

Max wanted to protest. Surely in the modern world you could just stick an animal in a scanner or something and look at the images later over a cup of tea?

Max heard a wooden case open, polythene coverings being ripped off, fine metal instruments tinkling in racks.

'Lovely and sharp, bright and new . . .' Slynk was almost crooning over his array of knives.

What about X-rays? Max wanted to say. *That wouldn't hurt. Or a few intelligence tests? Put me in a maze. Or on a webcam.* Snake Diary — *that would be OK for a bit. You could study my droppings if you like . . . Just don't cut me open!*

'Now, where shall I begin?' Slynk muttered. 'I'd better get the head open for a start. Send a miniature camera in.'

Max began to flail about in desperation. But he felt determined hands grip the sack. Slynk suddenly pulled Max out and held him tightly behind the back of the head. It was a relief to have his fangs pulled out of the sack. But what would happen to him now?

'There's no escape, you little freak!' Slynk breathed. 'Soon it'll all be over!'

Slynk cackled and capered about the lab lining up his instruments and formulas, turning over pages of notes with his free hand. All the time he gripped

Max firmly with the other. Max had never seen his enemy like this before; Slynk seemed possessed of a strange fearlessness, a confidence he had never previously shown in dealing with living creatures.

The usual weaknesses, the fears, even the traces of common decency, had all vanished. Once Slynk set foot inside his laboratory, he showed a confidence Max had never seen in him before. This was Slynk's world: a world of technology and machinery, with no room for human or animal feelings. The set of brakes on this mad scientist's behaviour all failed at once. In his own environment, Slynk really seemed to be turning into Doctor Diabolical.

'I'll need to keep every vital organ in a separate, clearly labelled jar,' Slynk purred. 'Drain out the blood, pump the stomach, unravel the intestine and slice the skin up lengthways. That'll be the fun part!'

Max almost fainted. But this time, his cool reptile attitude came to his rescue. *Snakes are cunning, snakes are patient, snakes stay in command*, he said to himself.

Max started to feel better. 'Reptiles rule! They're wild and cool!': the words of Fred Flinders, the cheery zoo guide came back to him. He would stay cool, he promised himself. No matter what.

There was a system that Uncle Herbert had for staying calm, for not being overwhelmed by worries. It was his Bottom Line System. Basically, it worked like this: whatever was worrying you, no matter how bad it seemed – a tough exam; a row with a best friend; a rotten hair cut, you name it. Whatever worried you, the bottom line was, *Will this actually kill me?*

Comfortingly, the answer had always been, *No*. Until now.

7. Venomous Villainy

It's now or never, Max thought to himself. *I'm a mighty python – I can take this guy! A wriggle, a pounce, a swift bite . . .*

He tried to pull himself together. He remembered what had happened the last time he had bitten something – he'd been trapped in the sack by his own teeth!

But surely this was different. He wasn't in a mad rage any more – he had overcome that. Now he was thinking of biting Slynk as part of a proper, sensible plan. Then, he had been trapped in the car boot. Now he was in a big, rambling laboratory – and his snake instincts told him this was good news.

There must be hundreds of cracks and holes here to slip into, Max thought. He knew that a snake – even a large python – only needed a tiny crack to poke its head into, and it was away. It could squeeze its whole amazingly flexible body through as well. *One bite and I'm free.*

Max was sure that Slynk couldn't really hold him prisoner with just one hand. Max hoped that, in his excitement, Slynk wouldn't notice the python's blue eyes. Max's eyes always stayed their natural colour whatever the transformation, and that was one fact he didn't want his enemy to find out.

Just bite him! Max reasoned.

It was tempting. And it would be very satisfying. After all the worry that Slynk had put him through, now it was payback time! Max's forked tongue flickered in and out in anticipation.

Suddenly, Slynk heaved Max over to a big wooden bench, still keeping that powerful grip behind the python's head. There before him, Max saw a jar with a latex membrane, a kind of soft, absorbent skin, covering it.

Max knew exactly what it was – and what was about to happen. With sudden, brutal force, Slynk shoved Max's head down into the jar.

'Go on,' growled Slynk through clenched teeth. 'Have a good bite. You know you want to!'

Max certainly did. His animal instincts were so outraged at this treatment he was ready to dig his fangs into just about anything.

'What's it like to be outwitted every step of the way?' Slynk crowed. 'No doubt you've been planning to give me a nasty dose of your venom? Lying there, acting all innocent. Well, I know about snakes and I know how to make them as harmless as garden worms!'

Slynk forced Max's head further into the jar, making the snake angrier.

'I'm going to milk all the venom out of you,' Slynk explained. 'It's child's play – I've seen it on TV! All your precious poison, the only weapon you've got against me, will be drained from you!'

If Max hadn't been so furious, he would have found the whole thing hilarious. Typical Slynk! He had seen one documentary about snakes and thought he knew everything. The half-baked boffin didn't realise that pythons have no venom at all.

Even Max, who hardly paid any attention to his parents' endless lectures on wildlife, knew how pythons overwhelmed their prey. He had seen it on TV and in comic strips, the mighty snake wrapping its coils around its victim, and then

squeezing, tightening its grip just enough to stop its prey breathing.

Max wondered what his parents would think of Professor Slynk if they could see him now – milking a python! That would be a good chuckle for the Explorer's Club annual tea party. He also wondered what they'd have to say if they knew what was *really* happening to their son right now!

Suddenly, Max had a bright idea. He would pretend to struggle – make out that he was really desperate to escape from being milked. Then, Slynk would believe his plan was working. Max twisted his body from side to side and flailed about with his tail, putting on a show of futile anger.

'That's it, pit your feeble strength against me!' cackled Slynk. 'I enjoy a good laugh!' He thrust Max's head deeper into the jar. Now was the time. Max opened his jaws with relish and bit deeply into the soft fabric.

'Yes!' rejoiced Slynk. 'It worked! Get stuck in, you fanged freak! It's milking time!'

It was a deeply satisfying feeling. As his fangs cut deeper into the latex, Max experienced the savage joy a wild creature feels at striking out, using the ferocious fangs nature has given it. This was better than finding a rare football card or working a cheat in a tough computer game! It almost made Max hiss with laughter to imagine what Jake would think if he knew that his best friend now preferred biting to computer games. But best of all, the biting action made Max dribble saliva into the jar – tons of it! There was not a trace of poison in it, but Slynk was hardly going to check that out.

For the first time since he had been taken prisoner, Max started to cheer up. He was pleased to be lulling his enemy into a false sense of security. With the supposed venom now out of the way, Max could sense Slynk beginning to relax, becoming just a bit too confident.

Max put on a final feeble wiggle just for show, then Slynk pulled the snake's head out of the jar.

'There! Completely harmless! The deadly jungle predator becomes as scary as a lump of old sausage.'

Max rolled his blue eyes, and gave the best withering look he could manage, considering that – with a python's limited features – he had the face of an angry sock puppet.

Poison sac or no poison sac, a huge python isn't exactly harmless – as Slynk was about to find out. Max saw no point in biding his time any more. Now, while Slynk still had him gripped with just one hand, was the moment to test his strength.

One twist with all his might, one savage snap of his jaws and Slynk would faint clean away!

But then, disaster. Just as Max was about to act, Slynk whipped him off the bench and stuffed him into a tank on the floor below. Before Max could use his full strength to fight back, he had been squashed into an incredibly tight space. A wooden lid was jammed on top. Max could hardly move.

It must be against the law to keep a snake my size in a poky prison like this, Max hissed feebly to himself, like a punctured bike tyre.

That was something else to add to Slynk's list of crimes. But Max had a horrible feeling that the deranged professor's biggest crime was about to take place.

Slynk heaved the tank on to a table, then bustled out of view. Max was starting to panic. He had to know what was going on. With a painful contortion, Max managed to force his head along the inside of the glass pane and into a position where he could see his foe. There was Slynk, rummaging around in the equipment room next door.

Max's blue eyes brightened with hope for a moment. Slynk was changing his clothes! Was he going out? Would this be a chance for Max to catch his breath and plan his getaway?

But then Max realised the horrible truth. Slynk was donning a white lab coat, taking off

his thick protective gloves and slipping on thinner surgical ones.

Time was running out.

8. In the Tank

Max peered around him. Was this the last sight he would ever see? The scalpels glinted on the table ready for use. Sample bottles stood open, sterilised and labelled, ready for his bits to be plopped into each one.

He looked at the walls of the lab. For the first time he noticed the sinister contraptions on the shelves all around him. There were half-finished robots, insect-like bodies on toy tank tracks, miniature cameras stuck on to the heads of

clockwork dolls. There was the skeleton of a rat wired up to a device that made it open and shut its bony jaws. And there was a tiny animal brain floating in a jar, connected by wires to a computer.

You're next, Max told himself.

In years to come people would see a python lolling around lifelessly in a huge glass bottle, and they'd say, 'Oh, what a fascinating specimen, how unusual to find a python with blue eyes!'

I'm not giving up yet, Max resolved, grimly.

He tried to think, but he kept seeing those bright blades, wondering which one would cut him open. His eyes glanced up at a camera sited above the operating table and he felt sick, throughout the length of his stomach. Slynk was going to make a film of Max's demise and probably put it on the Internet, or make a documentary about his research. Max had always wanted to be on TV – but not like this!

A whole series of 'what ifs' crowded into Max's mind, driving him mad. What if Jake hadn't wanted to see a transformation? What if Mr Knocker hadn't organised a trip to the zoo? What if he had changed into something else? He would have liked to see Slynk try and smuggle a rhino out of the zoo.

The worst thing of all was the thought that Molly and Jake – and his parents – would never even know what had happened to him!

Professor Slynk came back into view, reached up and adjusted the lens of his video camera. Then he came up close to the tank and stared into it intently. Those dark, beady eyes made Max's scales crawl. What was he looking for?

Still staring, the professor reached slowly into his pocket. Max quaked. What was Slynk up to now?

The professor pulled out a greasy comb, and ran it through his wispy fringe. Max let out a great hiss of relief.

He's not staring at me, Max realised. *He's looking at his own reflection in the tank! He's combing his hair because he's about to film himself, the vain old twit!* Pausing to tug out a stray nose hair, the professor waddled away again.

It was all too ridiculous. Max decided then and there that he was not going to die. Not like this – on a table in a stinking lab, at the hands of a stupid, evil man!

Now he could hear a strange tuneless noise, vibrating through the table and setting his nerves on edge. What weird form of torture was this? He looked into the next room and saw it was only Slynk singing.

It was a loathsome sight. Insanely happy because he had finally got what he wanted, the stocky little man was dancing around in his dissection outfit, wailing out snatches of his favourite cheesy old disco tunes.

Nothing could be worse than this, Max groaned.

'Of course, I won't be needing you any more!' Slynk suddenly said, bringing his partying to a halt. 'You'll be on the scrap heap!'

What is Slynk on about now? Max wondered.

He's talking to himself. Maybe he's going mad! Max looked closer, and then realised that Slynk was addressing his little robot spies. They were in a plastic tub on a shelf, ambling about brainlessly.

'You've served me well in your own feeble, slavishly loyal way,' Slynk went on, holding one in the palm of his hand as if it were a pet. 'But frankly you're past it, you're no use to me now. And what Slynk doesn't need gets trashed!' With a superior smirk, Slynk tossed the robot into a nearby bin.

How pathetic, Max thought. *Lording it over his own toy robots. If only this was going on the webcam, it would make the professor look a right saddo!*

'I won't have to try and sell you lot to the ignorant espionage industry, or the Spy Shopping Channel any more! I'll be rich!' he raved. 'Rich! And did you ask me why?'

Max pulled a sour face. *No, they didn't ask you why! They can't talk, because you made such*

rubbish robots. Slynk, however, raved on.

'Then I'll tell you why!' cried the professor. 'Because once I crack the secret of human-into-animal transformations, every government in the world will come crawling to me for my services!'

Now Max had to admit he was getting interested. He knew his powers were pretty special but why did Slynk think they were so important?

'Imagine a man who could command a plague of locusts! Imagine a navy of killer whales controlled by human brains, ruling the seas! Or consider perhaps, one tiny mosquito assassin carrying one deadly drop of infection into the right presidential home?'

Max squirmed. Slynk really did have dangerously insane visions. He had to be stopped. Not just for Max's sake, but for the sake of the world!

Through the glass, Max eyed his captor. What

a revolting specimen of humanity! Max sneered at Slynk and his reptile lips slid back over his rows of sharp teeth. Compared to Slynk, a snake was an admirable creature.

Maybe I'm going about this all wrong, Max thought to himself. *Up till now I've been forgetting that I'm more than just a boy in the body of a snake — I really AM a snake!*

Starting to flex all his muscles and explore the strength of his tightly wound coils, Max felt a power surging through him.

I have to use all the snake's wiles and abilities to get out of this mess, he told himself, *stop thinking like a boy, and start to actually BE a snake!*

Max looked down at his long body. He was a seriously big snake. A beauty. But there was more to a snake than just its looks. A python could also be a strong, proud animal, capable of using serious muscle.

Max coolly examined the tank he was packed into. It had a glass front and three wooden sides. It was no good just pushing at the glass, he needed to burst it open using all of his strength.

Max tensed his muscles and started to expand his python body.

9. Smashing Time

Max put everything into his one big, life-saving effort. When Slynk had first squashed Max into the tank, Max had been horrified by the lack of space, the feeling of being packed in. Instinctively, his elastic body had contracted, shrunk, making as much room for himself as possible.

Now Max had to do the opposite. It was time to think big. He rippled his muscles and pushed outwards. He could feel his long body go stiff, his coils hardening. He gritted his four rows of teeth, picturing himself expanding like a pile of tyres.

His scales were now pressing up against the four walls of the tank, there was scarcely room for an ant to move in there.

Nothing happened.

Keep going, something's got to give, Max told himself, *and it mustn't be you.*

After the strain of keeping himself contracted for so long, this powerful push outwards was a glorious feeling. He made himself as hard as rock.

Come on, Max told himself. *This is living, reptile strength versus some cheap old tank Slynk probably bought in a junk shop. Keep pushing!*

Then it came. At first just a tiny groan, an infinitesimal splintering of the glass wall. But to Max it was sweet music. The tickling of the vibration against his skin told him what that sound meant.

With an almighty smash, the whole tank split apart, its glass front hitting the floor and shattering into hundreds of bits.

There was a cry from Slynk in the next room. Max shot across the table, on to the floor and under a large cupboard. Slynk dashed in, just microseconds too late, to see where Max had gone.

Slynk went crazy at the sight of the shattered tank, cursing and ranting in disbelief. Max stayed

under the cupboard, his heart pounding.

But then he heard a most unwelcome sound. A nasty little giggle. Slynk had taken his face out of his hands, stopped gnashing his teeth, and was laughing.

'So the clever little snake got out of his box,' Slynk snickered. 'Well, you may not have noticed, but this lab is just another, slightly bigger box!'

He whipped round and locked the door to the next room.

'And it's a box with solid brick walls – and no way out!' he almost shrieked the last words, as he shoved a stool aside, knocked some boxes over and kicked a bin across the floor, trying to catch a glimpse of Max.

Max's cold-blooded response was to remain even more still. A python fighting for its life was not going to be startled into movement.

Now you have a chance. Don't waste it! Max's

instincts told him. Slynk might still be laughing and confident, but the odds on his own survival had suddenly improved. For the first time in hours, he wasn't a prisoner. He might still be inside his enemy's lab but he was free to act – free to strike back.

Slynk came prowling around the room, pushing aside bookcases and workbenches as he tried to flush Max out. Books and test tubes were shaken to the floor, one specimen jar hit the ground and shattered – a pale pickled rat lay in a pool of stinking fluid.

The professor pulled a disgusted face and stopped. He reached over into a corner and grabbed a cardboard box, emptying its contents on to the floor.

'Why waste energy hunting you down myself?' he smirked. 'I can get my latest inventions to do it for me!'

Out swarmed a new generation of Slynk's spy robots. From his hiding place under a heavy fridge, Max saw the tiny, multi-legged metal drones scatter across the floor like mad crabs and claw their way towards him.

Whereas Slynk was a big, slow-moving object, easy to evade in this deadly game of hide-and-seek, the robots were just the right height to creep under the furniture and probe the dark places where a python could curl up and hide.

Max had to move fast. The miniature cameras on the battery-powered bugs were zooming in on him. What was that shape? It had many of the characteristics they had been programmed to recognise … *Bleep, bleep!* Like angry watch alarms, the robots signalled their discovery and scurried closer.

Max slithered out from under the fridge and started squeezing himself under a dusty radiator.

93

He was too slow. Several robots had attached themselves to his scales and were now flashing their red lights as well as squealing with electronic excitement.

In desperation, Max lashed his tail and sent the bugs flying. They whipped through the air, catching Slynk in the face. He whimpered as their tiny legs scratched and stung his baby-smooth skin.

That was a stupid idea, Max thought. *Now Slynk knows where I am!* A mob of robots blocked his way back under the fridge. Puffing and beetroot-faced from the thrill of the hunt, Slynk advanced towards Max armed with a syringe. Max didn't know what was in it, but he could guess it would mean one thing for him – curtains. Suddenly, he felt terrified.

You can take this guy any day, you're a huge, powerful snake, Max told himself. Slynk crept forwards slowly, closing down Max's escape options.

94

Suddenly, Max was filled with a desire to stand up and fight. Was he about to change back to a boy again? To be human and plant two firm feet on the ground and give Slynk a knuckle sandwich? No, it was too soon, Max felt no tingling sensation as yet, no sign that he was transforming.

He reared up. Slynk had only seen him subdued before, tightly coiled or meek and helpless. He had never seen Max in his full glory, a monstrous, glistening serpent – a true terror of the jungle – rising up in deadly anger.

Give him the works! Max told himself. He opened his jaws and let out the most menacing, blood-curdling hiss Slynk had ever heard. The professor paused, just for a moment, uncertain of himself. Then he raised his syringe, glanced at the venom jar on the table and guffawed.

'Nice try! Why not play a bluff when you've

got no other hope left?' he laughed. 'But you can't hurt me and you know it!'

Slynk rushed forwards with the syringe. This was it. Max had to do something. Knowing he wasn't poisonous, Max arched his upper body backwards to maximise his striking speed. Then, at the last moment, he hurled himself at his enemy and, with all his strength, sank his fangs into Slynk's thigh.

10. Reptile Rage

Slynk gasped and dropped the syringe. His eyes glazed over, then closed as he toppled to the floor, his huge body crunching down on his own little robots, the shattered glass and the pickled rat.

Yesss! Max hissed to himself, experiencing a deep reptilian satisfaction at a nasty job well done. He felt a thrill of relief run the length of his body, to have escaped the death sentence that had been hanging over him for the past few hours.

Then Max realised he was feeling more than

relief, he recognised the familiar tingle that meant he was turning back into a boy. As a strange taste swamped his mouth, he checked to make sure that the professor wasn't moving. Thankfully, his enemy was still out for the count, stunned by the shock of Max's mega-bite.

Max's vision blurred and the full transformation started to overcome him. He felt his body swelling, his lungs puffing up, his scales bubbling and limbs sprouting from his sides. His scalp prickled and pale blonde hair began to flow out. He blinked with relief to have his eyelids back and, despite the pain, he grinned with delight as his teeth regrew.

He smiled even more seeing Slynk lying on the floor among the shattered glass like a beached whale. No, that was unkind to whales. Slynk just looked like a big, repulsive human.

But there was no time to gloat. Tasting a salty tang in his mouth, he wiped his lips and saw the smear of red on his fingers – Slynk's blood. Max grimaced. Was it biting a human being that had left him feeling sick, or was it just nervous exhaustion? He wondered if he'd ever tell anyone the full story of his incredible day out.

There was no time to hang around, Slynk could wake up again at any moment. Delighted to have arms, hands and fingers again, Max dug into the discarded old sack, pulled out his school clothes and dressed as quickly as he could, not bothering to put on his socks under his shoes. Then he shot back the bolts of the heavy lab doors and ran for his life along the echoing grey corridors of The Academy.

Rounding a corner at top speed, he almost knocked a startled handyman from his stepladder before he ducked out of a side door, sprinted across a courtyard garden, jumped over a low fence and hit the street still running.

The school was several streets away and, amazingly, Max dashed through the gates just seconds before his coach arrived back in the car park.

Max slowed down to a walking pace and finished buttoning up his shirt. Trying to look cool, he waved at Jake and was rewarded with a huge, relieved grin as his pal tumbled down the coach steps.

'I was so worried. You just disappeared and I couldn't find you anywhere.' Jake lightened up a little knowing his friend was safe. 'I'm guessing I missed the whole thing!' He handed over Max's spare parcel of clothes. 'So what happened?'

'First things first!' Max said quietly. 'Did anyone miss me? Did anyone see the change?'

'No one saw anything,' replied Jake, 'least of all me! Your secret's still safe.'

'What about my disappearance? Is it the talk of the coach?'

'No,' said Jake. 'I answered for you when Mr Knocker called out your name. I think someone else was the talk of the coach . . .'

Max looked up as a gale of laughter swept through the crowd of pupils at the school gate. Emerging last of all, marched along by a grim-faced Mr Knocker, was Stewart Staines, his school uniform stained orange with chimpanzee poo.

There was pandemonium. For the students who had had to put up with Brain Strain's moronic reign of terror, this was the biggest event of the term.

To his surprise, Max went almost misty eyed. For a moment he felt a wave of affection for his friends and his everyday life. To think he might never have lived to see this hilarious scene.

Max was still shocked at the horrible lengths Slynk had been prepared to go to, to discover the secret of Max's power. He hoped that once the professor had recovered from his bump on the head, he would feel disgusted at his own actions and change his evil ways. *Dream on!* Max said to himself. *Like that's ever going to happen!*

'This has made me realise, my ability is more awesome than I ever thought before!' Max raved to his pal as they raced towards Jake's house now that school was over.

'I just have to ask one more time. Is all this transformation stuff real? You're not just having me on, are you?' Jake eyed Max narrowly, 'I still haven't actually seen anything!'

Max laughed.

'I'll surprise you one day. Just for now I'm glad to be human again. I mean, how can you open a crisp packet without hands? That's pretty tough on a python!'

They stopped off at the shop. Max was in urgent need of some sweet chilli 'n' cheese nachos.

'You should ask them if they've got dead mouse flavour!' Jake laughed. 'That's what snakes eat, isn't it?'

Max chuckled. The best thing about having adventures was definitely talking about them afterwards! He enjoyed every moment of spilling his horror story to Jake, watching his friend gasp and groan along to every detail. Jake laughed until tears came out of his eyes as Max impersonated Slynk's waddling attempts at disco dancing. In fact, Max had some trouble getting Jake to listen to the rest of his story. His friend was too busy 'doing the Slynk'.

'He's talking about creating a fleet of human-minded killer whales. Or using mosquitoes to carry diseases and work as hit-men!'

They laughed and laughed, until they realised it actually wasn't funny at all. Then they laughed again anyway.

Jake became thoughtful and pulled a disgusted face.

'I'm trying to imagine what it's like – being a snake, wriggling under that old fridge, in the dust and dirt, through the dried-up peas and chewed-off fingernails!'

'There's an up side to it too,' Max smiled. 'It feels so great to –' he stopped himself. He didn't want to talk about biting Slynk. That would remain Max's secret, for now.

'To what?'

'To have real fangs!' Max grinned, baring his teeth like a vampire.

'That is definitely the cool part,' Jake agreed.

'And you know, pythons have a great attitude! They're kind of sly and wise at the same time. True survivors. They can get mad, but hold it all back until just the right moment.' Max sighed. 'Maybe that's what it feels like being a grown-up,' he mused.

Jake shook his head. 'Take a look at Mr Knocker, Slynk and your Uncle Herbert! There's no up side to being a grown-up!'

They ran up to Jake's front door. Max was starting to feel safe again, the shadows of the day were melting away in the late afternoon sunshine.

'Dad's got a day off today,' Jake said. 'He's promised to make pizza. I expect after having those amazing fangs of yours you must be dying for a bite!'

Max groaned at the gag, but inside he couldn't feel happier. Slynk was out of action, for now, and Max was back in his own everyday world where the only diabolical thing to worry about was his best friend's sense of humour!

ore Sssplendid Sssnake Facts!

There are loads of them! There are about 2,500 species of snake.

Boffins love them! Snake boffins are called 'herpetologists'. The study of reptiles (snakes included) and amphibians is called 'herpetology'. So, now you know!

They lay eggs! Female pythons lay between 10 and 100 eggs at a time, which they keep them warm by moving their muscles in a sort of controlled shiver!

They can fly! Well, one of them can: the flying snake of southern Asia can glide from tree to tree while hunting for food.

They sometimes get scared! The reason rattlesnakes make a rattling noise is to frighten away attackers without having to use their venom. Some snakes survive by pretending to be other snakes; the non-venomous milksnake has the same colouration as the deadly coral snake.

Some are deadly! Large cobras are armed with 600 milligrams of venom – and less than 20 milligrams can kill a human!

Pythons can hunt in the dark! Most pythons have special, heat-sensing organs in their lower lip, allowing them to hunt their prey in complete darkness.

In case you don't already know, a snake in the grass is a sneak. Take this quiz to find out whether or not you have a snaky bone in your slithery little body . . .

Your little brother has accidentally got felt-tip pen on your parents' new duvet cover. Do you:

 Report to mummy immediately

B Use his 'crime' to get something you want from him

C Help him turn the duvet cover inside out and hope Mum doesn't notice

You know what your dad has bought your mum for her birthday. Do you:

A Say nothing – you shouldn't have been snooping in their wardrobe anyway

B Tell your mum you know what she's got and tease her by not telling her what it is

C Get her to give you more pocket money in exchange for the information

Your friend tells you he hasn't revised for his maths exam. Do you:

A Keep quiet

B Make sure the maths teacher knows about it

C Tell anyone who'll listen!

...N THE GRASS?

You see your big sister kissing her boyfriend – the one your parents don't like. Do you:

A Pretend you didn't see

B Tell her you spotted them and see what she says

C Use the information to get her to buy you sweets

You think lying is:

A Extremely naughty – a lie would never escape from your lips

B Only allowed in absolute emergencies, and then only when it doesn't harm others

C Fine – you lie all day, every day

NOW CHECK YOUR SCORES

MOSTLY A S: Congratulations! You're an honest, trustworthy person. You can be a bit of a goody two-shoes though, which can get on the nerves of your less angelic mates. But, hey, nobody's perfect!

MOSTLY B S: You can be a bit sneaky and snaky and are in danger of becoming a fibber if you're not careful. Snooping is your favourite hobby, but remember that when you nose around the way you do, the only thing you're likely to get is into trouble. Big time!

MOSTLY C S: You're a snake in the grass to the max, a sneak extraordinaire! You can't keep a secret to save your life and you'd sell your granny for 5 pence. What are you like?!

UNCLE HERBERT'S SSSNAKE SSSNACK

Uncle Herbert did try swapping the cheese and cucumber for cold porridge and pickled gherkins, but it gave us stomach ache so he agreed to swap back!

YOU'LL NEED:

A long baguette/French stick

Some cream cheese

A cucumber

A pitted black olive

A red pepper

Some lettuce leaves

A grown-up helper

HERE'S WHAT TO DO:

1 Get your grown-up to do the following:
   - Cut the baguette into several slices, putting a horizontal slit into one end for the snake's mouth
   - Cut the cucumber into several slices too
   - Cut a long strip from the red pepper, making one of the ends forked (like a snake's tongue)
   - Top and tail the olive and cut two horizontal slices from the middle bit

2 Plaster both sides of each slice of bread with cream cheese

3 Stick a piece of cucumber between each slice

4 Press all the slices of bread together

5 Stick the snake's eyes on to the head using some cream cheese

6 Tuck the strip of red pepper into the horizontal slit to make a tongue

7 Decorate a plate with some jungle foliage (well, lettuce leaves!), and place your 'snake' on top, arranging it in a curvy shape

8 Share with friends!

YUM!

Can't wait for the next book
in the series?
Here's a sneak preview of

MONKEY MAYHEM

available now from all good bookshops, or
www.beastlybooks.com

1. Crackers Christmas

'I wonder what I'm getting for Christmas this year?' Max Murphy pondered aloud, while trying to scrape the final tiny crumbs of crisp out of a monster-sized packet. 'Oh, no, I don't,' he contradicted himself. 'I already know – two weeks in a creaky old, mosquito-filled safari lodge in Kenya, being terrorised by monkeys and bats!'

'Where's your sense of adventure?' buzzed his sister Molly as she picked up bits and pieces she needed to pack, whilst dancing around to her MP3.

'It's only an hour till we leave and we have to make sure we've got everything we could possibly need.'

'It's all right for *you*,' Max said, 'but think what it could be like for me in Kenya. With my special abilities I could end up transforming into a gazelle and being eaten by a lion.'

Just then, Uncle Herbert arrived in the room on roller blades, attempted a sharp turn and collapsed into an enormous bean-bag chair.

'You're a very lucky pair!' he said, shaking his mane of yellow hair out of his eyes. 'Other children get boring old CDs and DVDs and SIBs for Christmas, but you are getting a trip to Africa! Not everyone has parents who are compiling the ultimate animal encyclopedia.'

'That's true,' Molly grinned at Max, then swung back to Uncle Herbert. 'What on earth are SIBs?'

'Straight-In-the-Bins!' grinned her uncle. Max frowned. He was still wondering how much Uncle Herbert had overheard. Max and Molly had no plans to share the secret of his ability to transform into animals with any grown-ups as yet. Not until adults – as a species – had shown any sign they could be trusted.

'So we both think Max should stop moaning,' Molly agreed. She looked at the icy rain trickling down the window. It was nearly eleven and the sun didn't seem to have bothered to rise today. Kenya was definitely a much better place to be.

'Oh, I'm not suggesting he should stop moaning,' Uncle Herbert replied with a twinkle in his eye. 'I don't think children should ever be deprived of their favourite pastimes, it's bad for their development! Now who wants to stir the anchovies into the Christmas pudding with me? If we do that today it should be delicious round about, um . . . Easter!'

Max checked he had put all his favourite games and comics in his case for the fifth time.

'You almost seem glad to get rid of us,' Max sulked, resenting his uncle's cheery mood.

'I am working on a new book of puzzles at the moment,' he said. 'Pyramid puzzles. You build up triangles of hieroglyphics and if you get the answer wrong the curse of the pharaoh falls upon you. It's great fun!'

Max grinned. Uncle Herbert was getting kookier by the day. Maybe it was worth going to Kenya just to escape from whatever bizarre Christmas lunch he was planning to serve up. Last year's snowman-shaped cauliflower cheese with chocolate sauce had been disgusting.

It wasn't long before they were rushing through the lunchtime traffic to the airport, listening to the screeching of tyres, the furious honking of horns and the angry screams of pedestrians that always accompanied their uncle's driving.

'It's very tiring being given a lift by Uncle Herbert,' Max said as the pair boarded their flight for Africa. 'I always get arm-ache keeping my hands over my eyes.'

In contrast, their flight was wonderfully smooth, with spectacular views of beautiful cloudscapes, a funny movie and even tasty food.

'You know,' ventured Molly carefully, 'Kenya might not be as bad as you think.' She was treading dangerous ground, trying to get Max to admit that he might just be wrong.

'Maybe!' Max agreed, snuggling up in his inflatable neck-supporter and trying to grab a snooze. 'Maybe in Kenya cheeseburgers grow on trees and sisters stop nattering once in a while.'

Molly jabbed her elbow hard into Max's side.

'Not bad,' said Max, as they walked up the wooden steps of the Kilimanjaro Experience Lodge. 'Only a three-hour, bumpy bus-ride from the airport – I must be getting used to this globe-trotting lark.'

'Well you're in Amboseli National Park now,' replied Molly. 'So be careful which animals you look at, or you might be doing a different kind of trotting!'

They stepped from the bright sunshine into the shade of the lodge reception. There, among the elephant sculptures and tribal masks that were decorated with plastic holly, tinsel and fake snow – a welcoming committee awaited them. It included Mum, Dad and . . . Professor Preston Slynk! Slynk's pudgy body, squeezed into a crisp new safari suit, was leaning over the reception desk. Max went white, dropped his case and almost fainted.

'Wonderful to see you two!' Mrs Murphy said,

123

attempting to hug her offspring. 'What on earth is the matter with Max?'

Max pointed at Slynk, who was filling his name in at the desk. 'What is HE doing here?' Max blurted.

'Quite a spot of luck,' said their father. 'We just bumped into our old chum while on baboon-watch a few days ago. When he heard you two were joining us shortly, he said he simply must see you!'

The twins exchanged a grim look. Was there no escape from their arch-enemy?

'Slynk's the name,' the smarmy scientist was saying to the receptionist. 'It's spellt like "sly" but rhymes with "wink"!' He gave a wink as he said this, which made Molly feel sick.

'Rhymes with "stink", he means!' she muttered.

Slynk waddled over to join them. With his smooth, pink skin, tiny eyes and fine black hair he reminded Molly of an overgrown baby.

'At last!' Slynk gushed with pretend joy at seeing Max. 'It's been so long! You children have grown so much since the last time I saw you. Max has positively *transformed*!' he grinned, stressing the last word deliberately.

Same old Slynk, Max thought, gloomily.

'Let me show you your room,' said Mrs Murphy. 'There was rather a fine *phasmatodea* – that's stick insect – in my shower this morning. Perhaps you'll be lucky enough to have one too!'

While Mr and Mrs Murphy were looking the other way, Slynk glared at Max and Molly. Max's blood ran cold. The man was pure evil.

After a night's sleep, disturbed only by the whine of mosquitoes and the rooftop antics of black-faced monkeys, the twins were having a buffet-style breakfast on the shady veranda of the lodge, enjoying the breathtaking view of Mount Kilimanjaro.

'An all-you-can-eat buffet really wasn't meant for people like you, Max,' his mum sighed. 'Please leave some food for the rest of the guests!'

'We are so lucky to have reservations here!' Mr Murphy said. 'Amboseli National Park is three-hundred-and-ninety square kilometres of animal-watching heaven! There are over sixty major species here, including the fascinating yellow baboon!'

'Talking of baboons . . .' said Max, nodding towards Slynk, who was leaning on the veranda nearby, glancing around shiftily as if waiting for someone.

'Why has he got that enormous bag with him?' asked Molly. Her mum smiled.

'Surely it's obvious. Preston has very sensibly prepared an extensive first-aid kit. Medicines, syringes, forceps, sterilising equipment – as well as all the latest gadgets for monitoring brain waves and taking blood samples . . .'

Max kicked Molly under the table.

'That stuff is all to use on *me!*' he hissed at her. Their parents started to pore over a map, but Max kept watching Slynk. Two local men with sun hats pulled right down over their eyes came up to shake hands with him. Slynk swiftly handed over some bank-notes and waved them away.

'Professor Stink is *definitely* up to something!' Max whispered to Molly. 'We can't take our eyes off him for an instant!'